SEE HOW PLANTS GROW
Cereals

Nicola Edwards

PowerKiDS press.

New York

Published in 2008 by The Rosen Publishing Group, Inc.
29 East 21st Street, New York, NY 10010

First Edition

The publishers would like to thank the following for allowing us to reproduce their pictures in this book:
Alamy: 4 (Dinodia Images), 7 (David Lyons),
20 (Carol & Mike Werner/Phototake Inc), 22 (Dave King/dk), 23 (Nigel Cattlin/Holt Studios). Corbis: cover and 17 (First/zefa), title page and 13 (Michael S. Yamashita), 9 (Adam Woolfitt), 10 (photocuisine), 12, 16, 19 (Terry W. Eggers), 21 (Owaki-Kulla). Ecoscene: 6 (Martin Jones). FLPA: 14 (Nigel Cattlin), 18 (Holt Studios). Panos: 5 (Mark Henley), 8 (Jeremy Hartley). Still Pictures: 11 (Jim Holmes), 15 (Joerg Boethling).

Library of Congress Cataloging-in-Publication Data
Edwards, Nicola.
  Cereals / Nicola Edwards. -- 1st ed.
      p. cm. -- (See how plants grow)
  Includes index.
  ISBN-13: 978-1-4042-3702-5 (library binding)
  ISBN-10: 1-4042-3702-X (library binding)
  1. Grain--Growth--Juvenile literature. 2. Grain--Development--Juvenile literature. I. Title.
  SB189.E39 2007
  633.1--dc22
                              2006026535

Manufactured in China

Contents

What Are cereals?

Cereals are a group of plants that includes corn, rice, and wheat. Cereal plants produce **seeds** called grains, which we eat. Cereals are made into many different foods, such as bread, pasta, and noodles.

▼ In India, grains of rice are the first food a bride gives to her husband.

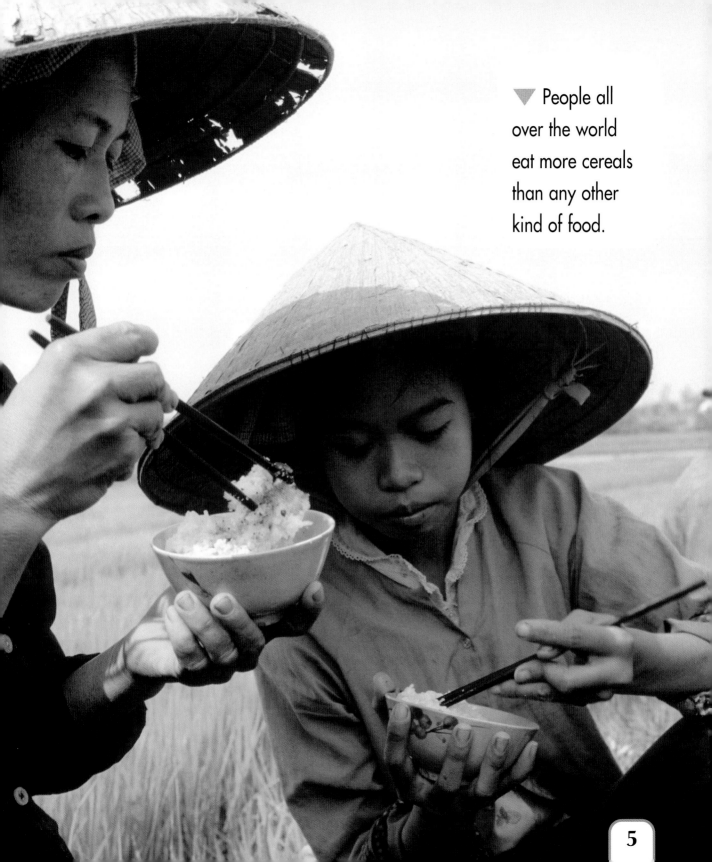

▼ People all over the world eat more cereals than any other kind of food.

Where do cereals grow?

People have grown cereals for food for thousands of years. Cereal plants can grow on small patches of land or in big fields. Many people across the world depend on cereals for food.

▼ Rice is an unusual cereal plant, because it grows underwater.

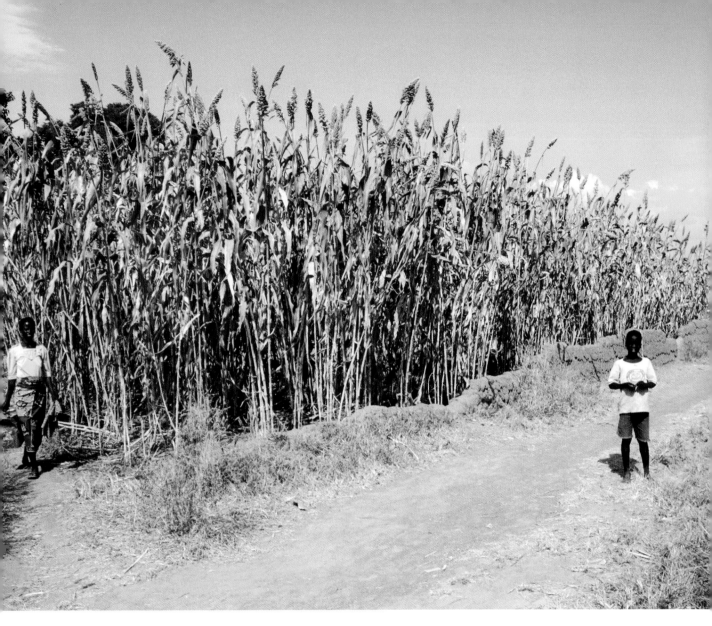

Plants such as wheat and rice are often grown on large farms. Some families in Africa grow cereal plants, such as millet, sorghum, or corn, outside their homes.

△ This field of corn belongs to a family in Nigeria.

Cereals around the world

Cereal plants are found in most parts of the world. They cannot grow in deserts, which are too dry, or at the North and South Poles, where it is too cold.

▼ This farmer is growing sorghum in Mauritania, northwest Africa.

Different cereals grow best in different **climates.** For example, sorghum and millet grow in hot countries, but wheat grows better in cooler temperatures.

▲ Oats are grown in areas that have a cool, damp climate, like Scotland.

What's in a grain?

A cereal grain is made up of different layers. A layer of **bran** covers the middle of the grain. The bran is rich in **fiber** and vitamins, which we need for good health. The center of the grain is high in energy-giving **starch**.

▲ Because each grain is full of **nutrients** for the new plant, it's good for us to eat, too.

Cereal Fact

In China, people greet each other by saying: "Have you had your rice today?"

The germ is inside this starchy center.
The germ is the part of the grain from
which new cereal plants grow.

▼ The outer
coatings of rice
grain are being
used as a **fertilizer**.

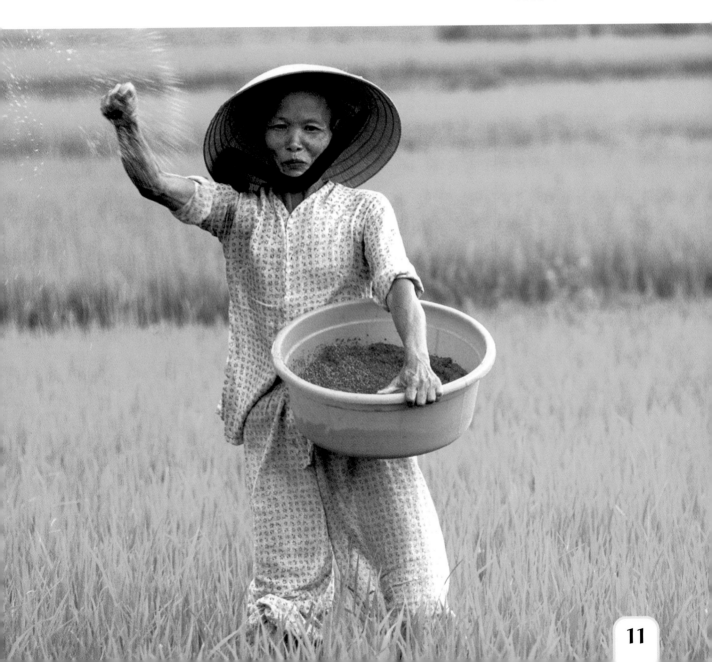

Planting seeds

Cereal plants are grown for food. Farmers prepare the ground to make sure the plants can grow well. They **plow** the fields where the seeds are to be sown. Paddy fields, where rice is grown underwater, are flooded before planting.

▼ This corn seed is germinating. Its **root** and shoot are beginning to grow.

Cereal Fact

Some countries plant cereal seeds by dropping them over large areas of fields from a plane.

Cereal seeds can be planted by hand or by machine. Seeds need to take in water before they can **germinate**, or start to grow.

▲ The rice seedlings in this paddy field are being planted by hand.

The growing plant

When a cereal plant starts to grow, roots grow down from the seed and spread through the soil. The roots take in water and nutrients from the soil for the growing plant. Most cereal plants are grasses, with long, thin leaves.

▲ Cereal leaves have a sheath wrapped around the stem and a thin, veined blade.

Cereal Fact
Grasses grow in an unusual way. When grass is cut from the top, it keeps on growing from underneath.

The leaves or blades of grass use sunlight, water, and air to make food for the growing plant.

▼ Can you see the roots on these rice plants?

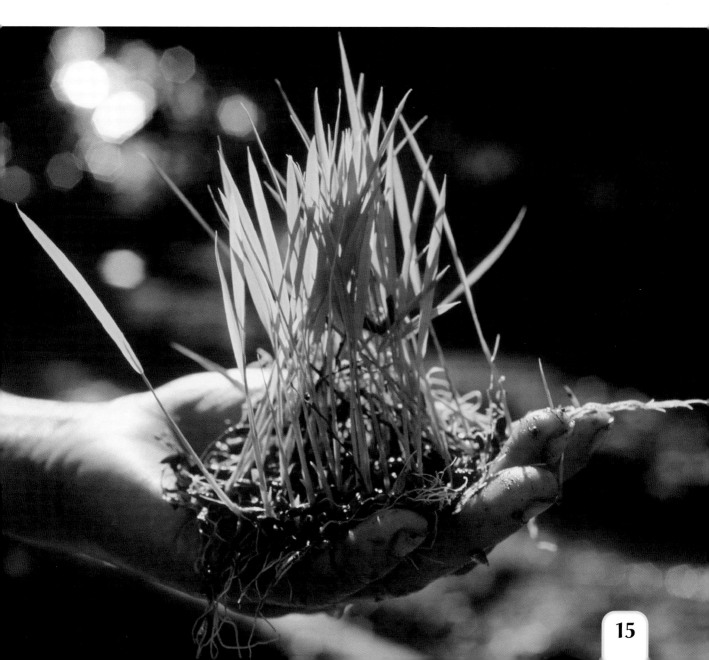

Flowers and seeds

As cereal plants, such as wheat and rice, grow, they develop **heads**. These heads contain the **flowers** of the plant. The flowers have male and female parts.

▼ This field of barley is in flower.

The male part of the flower produces **pollen**. When the pollen enters the female part, new seeds begin to develop.

▲ These heads of wheat have flowers inside them.

Harvesting cereals

Cereal plants change color from green to gold as their seeds **ripen**. When the seeds are ripe, they are ready to be gathered or **harvested**. Farmers harvest cereals by hand or by using powerful machines.

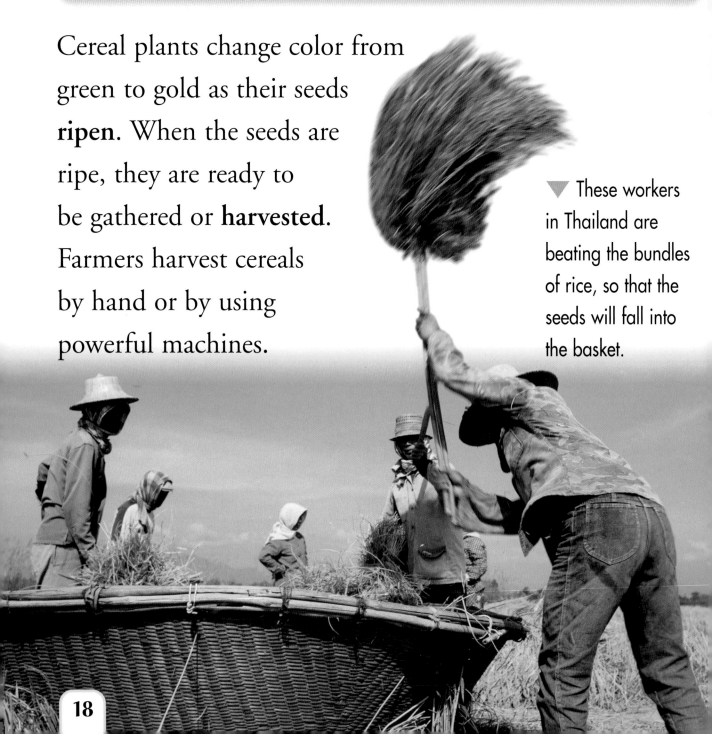

▼ These workers in Thailand are beating the bundles of rice, so that the seeds will fall into the basket.

After harvesting, farmers separate the grains from the rest of the plant. The grains have to be completely dry before they are stored. Otherwise they may rot.

This farmer in the Midwest is using a machine called a combine harvester to harvest the crop of wheat.

How do we use cereals?

People eat cereal grains, for example, as cooked rice or barley, or in porridge made from oats or sorghum. We also grind wheat and corn grains into flour.

How many foods can you think of that come from cereal plants?

20

The outer layers of rice grains can be burned as a fuel or turned into a fiber to make clothing.

▲ Cereal grains are used to feed farm animals, such as cows, pigs, and chickens.

Grow your own cereals

Plant some cereals, such as wheat or corn, and watch the plants develop. Soak the seeds in water overnight. Fill a container with soil. Gently push a few seeds into the soil until they are covered well.

▲ You could try planting different cereal seeds to compare how each type grows.

Cereal Fact

Rye is an unusual cereal plant, because it can grow in poor soil on high land.

Water the soil to keep it damp.
When do the leaves appear?
What do they look like?

▼ This wheat seed has germinated. A shoot is growing up from the seed while roots are spreading through the soil.

Glossary

bran
The outer layer of a cereal grain that is high in fiber.

climate
The types of weather that happen in different parts of the world.

fertilizer
A substance added to soil to help plants grow.

fiber
A substance found in plants that we eat to keep ourselves healthy.

flowers
The parts of a plant that produce pollen and from which fruits develop.

germinate
When a seed starts to develop into a new plant.

harvested
When a ripe crop is gathered from the place where it has been growing.

heads
The parts of a cereal plant that contain its flowers and in which seeds develop.

nutrients
Food in the soil that plants take in for growth.

plow
To prepare soil before seeds are planted in it.

pollen
The dustlike yellow substance produced by the male parts of plants and received by the female parts.

ripen
When a plant or a fruit becomes ready to be harvested or eaten.

roots
The parts of plants that anchor them in soil and take in water and nutrients.

seeds
The parts of a plant from which new plants develop.

starch
A substance found in some foods, such as cereals, that gives us energy.

Web Sites

Due to the changing nature of Internet links, PowerKids Press has developed an online list of Web sites related to the subject of this book. This site is regularly updated. Please use this link to access this list: www.powerkidslinks.com/shpg/cereal/

Index